To my sister, Liz, who is always there for me.
And Manny, too, of course. All my love —VMS

Especially for my Eleanor! —JS

The artist wishes to thank Susan Pearson, Melanie Donovan, and
Golda Laurens for their patience and inspiration; my everlasting thanks
to courtly T. R. Dryer, a fine friend and neighbor

HAPPY BIRTHDAY to ME!

BY
Valrie M. Selkowe

ILLUSTRATED BY
John Sandford

HarperCollins Publishers

It was an ordinary day

until I found a key

which opened the gate that led through the garden

to the great pink house

where the door opened

to let me inside

and the gray-striped cat holding the bright yellow box

with the shiny white ribbon

waited to take me

to the magical room

while the rocking horse rocked

and the lion did back flips as the monkey juggled

and the three little pigs squealed with delight

when they saw the cake with all of the candles

as we all started singing,

and the piano played my most favorite song:

Happy Birthday to Me!

Text copyright © 2001 by Valrie M. Selkowe
Illustrations copyright © 2001 by John Sandford
Printed in the U.S.A. All rights reserved.
www.harperchildrens.com

Library of Congress Cataloging-in-Publication Data
Selkowe, Valrie M.   Happy Birthday to me! / by Valrie M. Selkowe ;
illustrations by John Sandford.   p.   cm.   Summary: Through a
garden, inside a great pink house, a child discovers a wonderful birthday
celebration.   ISBN 0-688-16679-2 — ISBN 0-688-16680-6 (lib. bdg.)
[1. Birthdays—Fiction.   2. Animals—Fiction.]   I. Sandford, John, 1948—
ill.   II. Title.   PZ7.S456955 Hap   2001   00-29554   [E]—dc21

Typography by Carla Weise

1 2 3 4 5 6 7 8 9 10

❖

First Edition